Dear Parents,

Welcome to The Magic School Bus!

For over 20 years, teachers, parents, and children have been enchanted and inspired by Ms. Frizzle and the fabulous cast of beloved characters that make up The Magic School Bus series.

The unusual field trips, visual jokes, eye-catching details, and interesting information are just a few of the elements that make The Magic School Bus series an excellent tool to get your child excited about school, reading, and exploring their world.

It is important that children learn to read well enough to succeed in school and beyond. Here are some ideas for reading this book with your child:

- Look at the book together. Encourage your child to read the title and make a prediction about the story.
- Read the book together. Encourage your child to sound out words when appropriate. When your child struggles, you can help by providing the word.
- Encourage your child to retell the story. This is a great way to check for comprehension.

Enjoy the experience of helping your child learn to read and love to read!

Visit www.scholastic.com/magicschoolbus to subscribe to Scholastic's free parent e-newsletter, and find book lists, read-aloud tips, and learning hints for pre-readers, beginners, and older kids, too. Inspire a love of books in your child!

There are many Magic School Bus books for your reader to enjoy. We think you will enjoy these, too:

Ms. Frizzle

Liz

Written by Kristin Earhart
Illustrated by Carolyn Bracken

Based on The Magic School Bus® books
Written by Joanna Cole and illustrated by Bruce Degen

The author and editor would like to thank Ken Rubin for his expert advice in preparing the manuscript and illustrations.

ISBN 978-0-545-35685-5

12 11 10 9 8 7 6 5 4 3   12 13 14 15 16 17/0

Printed in the U.S.A.   40

First printing, January 2012

Designed by Rick DeMonico

The Magic School Bus® Inside a Volcano

Arnold   Ralphie   Keesha   Phoebe   Carlos   Tim   Wanda   Dorothy Ann

SCHOLASTIC INC.

New York   Toronto   London   Auckland
Sydney   Mexico City   New Delhi   Hong Kong

We are learning about volcanoes.
Tim made one out of clay.
He gets ready to set it off.

But Tim is not happy.
"This is just a toy," he says.
"I want it to work like a real volcano."
Ms. Frizzle says, "Let's go see one!"

There are always surprises with the Friz. When we get on the bus, it starts changing.

WHERE ARE WE GOING?

TO THE OTHER SIDE OF THE EARTH.

I GUESS WE'LL HAVE TO FLY.

DRILL!

9

13

We drill out of the core and through the mantle again.
Now we are on the other side of the earth.

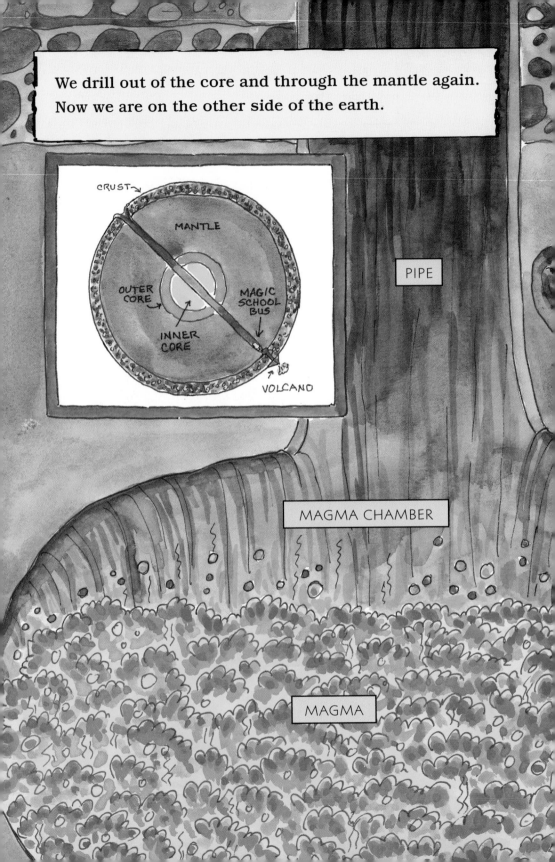

PIPE

MAGMA CHAMBER

MAGMA

We are close to the crust.
We are under a big volcano.
We see a giant, hot puddle.
Ms. Frizzle gives us heat-proof suits.

"Magma is very hot. These suits will protect you," says Ms. Frizzle.
Then she shouts, "Jump in, kids!"

WHAT IS MAGMA?
by Wanda

Magma is melted rock.
Magma is found in pockets inside the earth.
The pockets are under or within the earth's crust.

We look around.
The magma is rising higher.
The rumbling sound is getting louder.

WHAT WILL HAPPEN WHEN THE HOLE FILLS UP?

More magma fills the pocket.
It pushes us up.
We blast up into a tunnel.

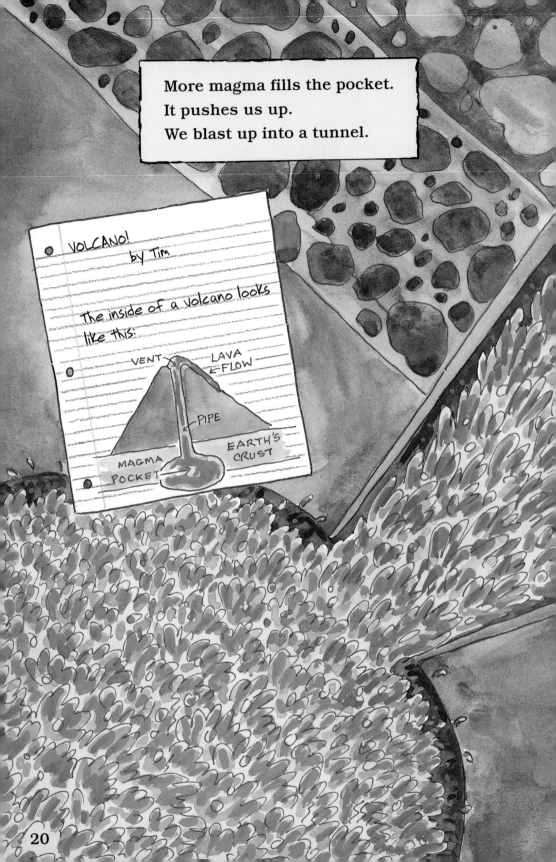

We shoot into the air.
We float on a thick cloud of ash.
Then the bus lands on a river of lava!

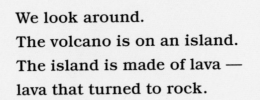

We look around.
The volcano is on an island.
The island is made of lava —
lava that turned to rock.

The Friz hits a button, and we lift into the air. Now the bus is the Magic School Helicopter.

WE'RE GOING UP!

WE'RE GOING AWAY!

HOORAY!

We fly over a lot of islands.
Ms. Frizzle says they are all volcanoes.

COMPOSITE CONE

SHIELD

CALDERA

CINDER CONE

Back at school, we make lots of models.
"There are different kinds of volcanoes,"
Tim says.
"But there is only one Ms. Frizzle."

31

LOVELY LAVA

Three common types of lava include:

Aa lava, which is thick and chunky. It can flatten most things in its path.

HOW TO SAY aa: AH-ah

Pahoehoe lava, which is thin and smooth. It looks like long ropes when it cools.

HOW TO SAY pahoehoe: pa-HOY-hoy

Pillow lava, which is rounded. It forms when underwater volcanoes erupt.

Aa and Pahoehoe are words in the Hawaiian language.

Q: What did one volcano say to the other?

A: I lava you!

I'M ERUPTING
WITH LAUGHTER!